Wa[...] and the Food Fair

by Linda Cernak
illustrated by Remy Simard

SCHOOL PUBLISHERS

Copyright © by Harcourt, Inc.

All rights reserved. No part of this publication may be reproduced or transmitted in any form or by any means, electronic or mechanical, including photocopy, recording, or any information storage and retrieval system, without permission in writing from the publisher.

Requests for permission to make copies of any part of the work should be addressed to School Permissions and Copyrights, Harcourt, Inc., 6277 Sea Harbor Drive, Orlando, Florida 32887-6777. Fax: 407-345-2418.

HARCOURT and the Harcourt Logo are trademarks of Harcourt, Inc., registered in the United States of America and/or other jurisdictions.

Printed in China

ISBN 10: 0-15-351513-9
ISBN 13: 978-0-15-351513-2

Ordering Options
ISBN 10: 0-15-351213-X (Grade 3 Advanced Collection)
ISBN 13: 978-0-15-351213-1 (Grade 3 Advanced Collection)
ISBN 10: 0-15-358103-4 (package of 5)
ISBN 13: 978-0-15-358103-8 (package of 5)

If you have received these materials as examination copies free of charge, Harcourt School Publishers retains title to the materials and they may not be resold. Resale of examination copies is strictly prohibited and is illegal.

Possession of this publication in print format does not entitle users to convert this publication, or any portion of it, into electronic format.

11 12 13 14 15 0940 12 11 10

Walter sat on the bus with his best friend, Heather. Today Ms. Perry told the class that they were going to hold a food fair, and pairs of students were assigned to bring in a food from a different country. Ms. Perry had let the pairs select countries out of a hat, and Walter and Heather had picked China.

"Do you think they eat hamburgers in China?" wondered Walter.

"I'm certain they do, but we're supposed to bring in a food that *comes* from China," replied Heather.

"Well, what about bananas? Do they eat those in China?" responded Walter

"Walter, will you please be serious?" exclaimed Heather.

"I am being serious," continued Walter. "I don't know anything about food from other countries, but I certainly know what I like!"

"Well, we absolutely have to pick a food that comes from China," replied Heather. "Then an adult will help us prepare that food, and we will bring it to the food fair so that everyone can taste it."

There was a great deal of excitement among the children about the food fair. They would learn about the countries where the foods came from, and then everyone would have a fantastic and delicious feast.

Unlike the other students, Walter was not looking forward to the fair because he didn't like to try new foods. He liked hamburgers, cereal, and bananas, and that was about it.

"Let's ask Lu Chen about Chinese food," suggested Heather. "He is from China, so he can give us some advice."

The next day at school, Walter and Heather found Lu Chen on the playground. "Hey, Lu Chen, what do they eat in China?" asked Walter.

"Well, there are lots of good foods," replied Lu Chen. "There are dumplings and noodles, and tons of rice, too."

"What country are you doing, Lu Chen?" wondered Heather.

"Christine and I are doing Mexico, so we are going to prepare tacos," replied Lu Chen.

"That sounds yucky," said Walter.

"Walter, you really must expand your thinking," Heather declared.

Heather and Lu Chen discussed the variety of foods that come from China. After much deliberation, Heather told Walter, "I think we should try to make egg foo yung!"

"Egg who what?" said Walter, looking very confused.

"It is an egg dish from China, and Lu Chen said his grandfather would be happy to help us," replied Heather.

"I'd better eat a sandwich before I go to this food fair because I'm sure I'm not going to want to eat any of the foods there," thought Walter.

During the next week, Walter and Heather worked on their egg foo yung recipe with Lu Chen's grandfather. They needed many ingredients for their dish. Lu Chen's grandfather cut up all the vegetables, and then Walter and Heather beat up the eggs in a big bowl. Finally, the whole mixture went into a hot pan. Walter had to admit it smelled delicious, and when it was cool enough to eat, it tasted delicious, too!

Finally, on Friday afternoon, family members began to arrive at school for the fair. Ms. Perry had done a thorough job of setting up the cafeteria. There was a big map of the world with circles on all the countries where the foods came from.

The kids were so excited they were almost ready to erupt. The students would give a short speech about their food, tell where it came from, explain what the food was called, and what ingredients were in it. After that, everyone would grab a plate, and the food tasting would begin!

Walter peeked at the foods on the tables and thought that some of them looked pretty horrible. There were pots with strange fish in them, thick stews spooned over steaming rice, and chunks of meat cut into cubes and speared onto sticks. Bowls held funny-looking vegetables, and pieces of chicken were sprinkled with some brown stuff. One dish contained bread that looked like pancakes.

"Doesn't it smell incredibly good in here?" asked Heather, looking at all the good food.

"I guess so, but Heather, there aren't any hamburgers!" wailed Walter. Walter looked around him and thought, "I'm sure to go hungry today."

The kids all gave the speeches about their foods, and then it was time for the tasting to begin.

At Lu Chen's table, Walter stared at the large plate of tacos, which had a grainy look to them.

Lu Chen's grandfather offered Walter a small piece, and he bit into the taco. It was warm and crunchy and, to his surprise, tasted quite good.

"What is inside of this?" Walter wanted to know.

"Oh, just some hamburger meat and stuff," replied Lu Chen.

"I didn't realize hamburger meat was used in other foods," said Walter.

Walter and his mother walked over to Shoshana and Anna's table. There on the table was a pot with some mysterious red sauce mixed with rice, shellfish, and meat. "What's this?" asked Walter, peering into the pot.

"It's food from Spain, and it's called paella [pä-ĕl'ə]," answered Anna.

Walter took a taste and exclaimed, "It's fish!"

"Don't you like fish?" said Anna.

"Well, it's okay, but I never had it in stew before. It actually tastes good," said Walter, licking his lips.

Paella
from Spain

Chapatti from Africa

Next, Walter and his mother moved over to Latrell and Doug's table, where they tasted chapatti, a type of flat bread from Africa. "Pretty good," said Walter as he took a bite.

At Lee and Jorge's table, they sampled a spicy chicken.

"It's a food from Jamaica called jerk chicken," explained Lee.

"Well, its certainly not as good as hamburgers — but not too bad either," declared Walter.

Finally, Walter and his mom reached Jeremy and Carla's table. "At last, spaghetti, a food I actually know!" said Walter.

Apple Pie
from
America

"So, Walter, what did you think of the foods?"
asked Walter's mother.

"I liked that so many foods had stuff in them that
I knew, and I actually liked the tacos, and the egg foo
yung we made!"

Then they came to the last table. Ms. Perry had
baked some apple pies.

"Well, I actually thought the food at the fair was
delicious, but there's nothing better than a piece of
apple pie!" said Walter, and he took a big bite.

Think Critically

1. How does Walter change during the story?

2. Using clues from the story, what does *deliberation* mean on page 7?

3. At what point in the story did you think that Walter would change his mind about tasting new foods?

4. What do you think the author wanted the readers to learn?

5. Which one of the foods in the story would you like to try? Explain.

 Science

Write a Recipe Think about a food you like. Write down all of the ingredients you think go into your recipe and try to figure out how much of each ingredient would be needed. Then look up the real recipe to see how close you are.

School-Home Connection Ask family members to name their favorite foods and to tell why they like them. What is your favorite food?

Word Count: 1,046